To Nnny nd Dvid. K.G.
For untie Cth and Uncle Mlc. J.F.

First published in 2016 by Hodder Children's Books

Text copyright © Kes Gray 2016
Illustration copyright © Jim Field 2016

Hodder Children's Books
An imprint of Hachette Children's Group
Part of Hodder & Stoughton
Carmelite House
50 Victoria Embankment
London EC4Y 0DZ

The right of Kes Gray to be identified as the author and Jim Field as
the illustrator of this Work has been asserted by them in accordance
with the Copyright, Designs and Patents Act 1988.

A catalogue record of this book is available from the British Library.

ISBN: 978 1 444 91956 1
10 9 8 7 6 5 4 3 2 1

Printed in China

An Hachette UK Company
www.hachette.co.uk

MIX
Paper from
responsible sources
FSC® C104740

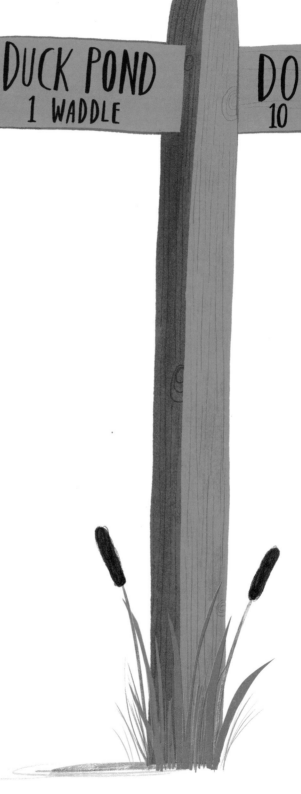

QUICK QUACK QUENTIN

KES GR Y
& JIM FIELD

Hodder
Children's
Books

Quentin was a duck with a very quick quack.

"QUCK!"

"And again," said the doctor.

Qu ck!

DOCTOR

"Mmmm," said the doctor.

"What's wrong with me?" qucked Quentin.

"It's simple," said the doctor,
"your QUACK has lost its A."

"Is there anything you can give me for it?"
qucked Quentin.

"I'm afraid not," said the doctor.
"As a DOCTOR, the only things I can give you
are a D, an O, a C, a T, another O or an R."

"I see,"
sighed Quentin.

DOCTOR

Quentin left the doctor's and went to the **FARM** to ask for an **A**.

"Hello," Quentin said to a group of animals who were gathered by the fence. "I was wondering if I might be able to have the A from your FARM."

"What do you need an A for?" asked the farm animals.

QU CK!

explained Quentin.

"We're sorry, Quentin," they said,
"we'd like to help you but if you have the **A** from
our **FARM** it won't be a **FARM** any more.
It will be a **FRM**. We don't think the **FARMER**
would want to be a **FRMER**."

"I understand,"
sighed Quentin.

"I'll give you my O if you like," woofed the DOG.

"Really!" said Quentin.

"No problem at all," the DOG replied.

Quentin took the O from the DG and tried it out.

QUOCK!

"You do sound a bit better," said the DG. "But you don't really sound like a duck."

"You can try my E if you wish," clucked the HEN.
Quentin took the E from the HN and tried that out.

"You still don't really sound like a duck," said the HN.

"Try my I," oinked the PIG.

But it was no good.

"Sorry, Quentin," said the farm animals, "nothing we can give you helps you sound like a duck."

Quentin sighed, thanked the farm animals and went to the ZOO.

Quoock!

said Quentin,

standing outside the Z gates

and trying out both of the Os.

But **quoock** sounded as odd as **quock**, **queck**, **quick** and **quuck**!

Quentin went to find some animals with **A**s.

All the zoo animals with As were very sympathetic, but there was one big problem...

The APES didn't want to be PES,

APES

the SNAKES didn't want to be SNKES,

SNAKES

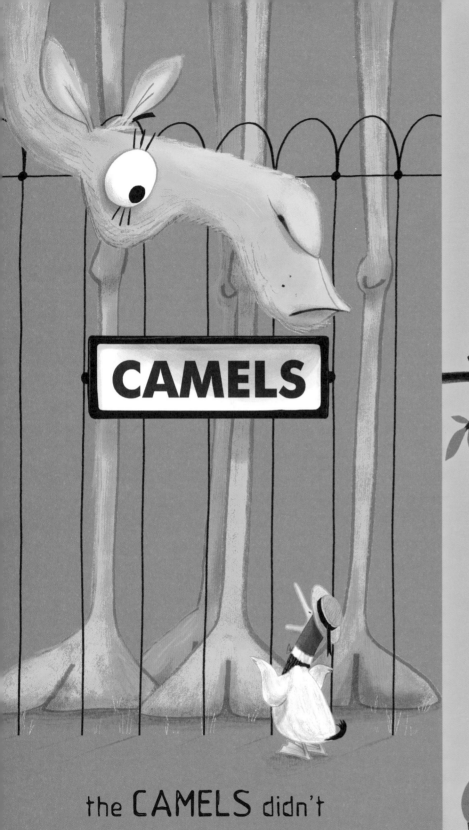

CAMELS

the CAMELS didn't
want to be CMELS,

PARROTS

the PARROTS
didn't want to be
PRROTS,

and the PANDAS didn't want to be PNDAS or even PANDS!

"It's hopeless," qucked Quentin, waddling glumly back towards the zoo gates. "I'm a duck with a QUICK QUCK and there's nothing anyone can do about it."

"I can do something about it,"
said a voice. "You can have
one of my As if you like.
I've got three."

Quentin looked up at the strangest
looking animal he had ever seen...

"What kind of animal are you?" qucked Quentin.

"I'm an AARDVARK," said the strange-looking animal,
"and I've got far more As than I need. Help yourself."

AARDVARK

Quentin took the first A
from the AARDVARK
and excitedly tried it out.

QuACK!

"It works!"
Quentin cried.

ARDVARK

Quentin gave the first A back and swapped it for the second A.

QUACK!!

"That A works too!" shouted Quentin.

"Works for me as well," smiled the ARDVARK. "Take your pick, Quentin!"

A RDVARK

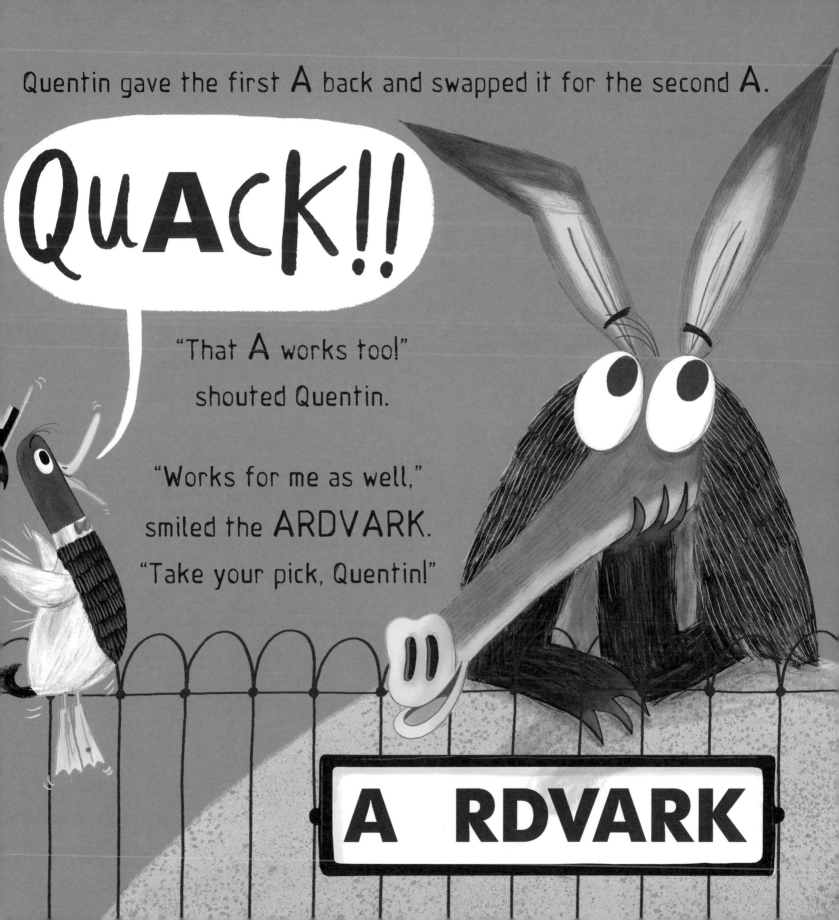

"I'm cured!" whooped Quentin. "Listen to my wonderful quack!"

QUACK!
QUAACK!!
QUAAACK!!!

"Don't be greedy now," laughed the RDVRK.